Redemption

To Randy

Hope you enjoy the book.

Scott Mead

To order additional copies, please contact us.
BookSurge, LLC
www.booksurge.com
1-866-308-6235
orders@booksurge.com

Redemption

The Angel of Death Book I

Scott Meador

Cover Art by Sharon Bauman

2005

Redemption

For my loving wife Belinda for believing in me enough to make me believe in myself.

PREFACE

In the annals of the American west, few legends loomed larger than that of The Angel of Death, J.T. Winters. Considered to be one of the fastest guns to have ever lived, the mere mention of his name was enough to strike fear into the hearts of the bravest of men. His speed and accuracy with his trademark duel Navy Colts was only matched by his ability to face seemingly insurmountable odds and to always find a way to come out on top.

Tales of his deadly deeds during the range wars of Texas and in various cow towns throughout the west placed him in the same regards as such legendary figures as Wild Bill Hickcock, Wyatt Earp, and Jesse James. Young boys throughout the country would draw their wooden pistols and pretend to be the Angel of Death facing down six men at once on the streets of San Antonio.

The only thing more legendary than his abilities was his disappearance. Everyone had a theory on the demise of J.T. Winters. Most believed that he had finally been bested by a young gun hand looking to make a name for himself. However, no one ever stepped forward to claim to have faced off with the Angel of Death and lived to tell the tale. So the question remained, whatever happened to the deadliest man who ever lived?

CHAPTER I

James Snow had been working for several hours before the sun began to peak up over the eastern horizon giving a dark orange glow to everything in sight. He had already milked the cow, gathered the eggs, and put both in the kitchen for Kaye. He was just finishing up with the repairs to the gate when he heard the love of his life calling him to breakfast. James checked the gate to make sure that it would hold, then dropped his tools and headed for the small log cabin across from the barn.

As he opened the door the smell of fresh biscuits, eggs, and coffee washed over him; he suddenly realized how hungry he was. James walked over and gently kissed Kaye on the lips as he picked up a cup of steaming coffee. Every morning he was amazed at how the mere site of his wife made his heart beat faster. James then turned to the table and patted Mark on the head before taking his seat. "Morning, squirt." The toddler giggled and slapped the tray of his highchair with both hands playfully.

"What are you working on this morning," Kaye asked as she placed the breakfast on the table.

James reached for a biscuit, "Just trying to fix that gate the bull pushed over. I swear I'll be glad when it is time to trade bulls with Stevens. That big Holstein has been nothin' but trouble since we got him." Once a year James traded bulls with Bill Stevens to keep his cattle's bloodline clean.

"Well, at least he gave us some good calves this year. We only lost two and that is a lot better than last year," Kaye said, looking on the bright side as always. The bull that they had used the year before had fathered some weak and sickly caves. Almost a quarter of the ones born had died within a month.

Five years ago, James would have never believed that one day he would be having a discussion with his wife about their cattle. He and Kaye had been married for four years, but to James it only seemed like a few short months. James had seen her working in the garden on her father's farm while he was passing through on a cattle drive headed for Abilene. The trail boss had sent him ahead to scout for water when he came across the small spread. When Kaye's father asked him what he needed, James stumbled over his answer because he was so smitten with her that he had almost forgot.

James had never seen anything as beautiful in his entire life. Her golden blond hair and big brown eyes literally took his breath away. Until that moment, James had never considered settling down and getting married, but he knew that Kaye would be worth it. He finished the cattle drive, collected his pay, and rode back south to find her again.

Kaye had pretended not to know why he had returned, but her father made it obvious that he knew it was not for the job that James had asked him for. The old man had seen enough men in his time to know that James was a rough one. The scar on his cheek and the two Navy Colts that he carried slung low did not bother him as much as the scar around his neck that James tried to keep covered with a bandana. Kaye's father had seen a scar like that once before. It was on the neck of a man who had been hanged, but was lucky enough to live to tell about it.

But after six months of hard work and persistence, James was beginning to win the old man over. James and Kaye had grown very fond of one another in the time he had spent on their farm, and when the old man caught the fever and died suddenly, no one was surprised when the two of them married shortly after. It had taken some convincing on James' part to get Kaye to pack up her belongings and move north, but James wanted to get as far away from the rest of the world as possible.

They found a good piece of land and started a little farm. James put away his guns and turned his back on his old life. He told Kaye that he had been in the war and afterwards had worked on cattle drives and other odd jobs. It was not a lie; it just was not the whole truth. James always suspected that Kaye knew that there was more to the story, but she never asked. Not even about the scar on his neck. A year later, Mark was born, and their little farm had grown until it was big enough to support them and to provide a few extras to trade for what they were not able to grow.

James finished his breakfast, kissed Kaye, told Mark to mind his mother, then headed back outside. He gathered his tools and went to the barn to fix the leaking roof. It always seemed as if something around the farm needed to be repaired, and James had grown to be a fairly good handyman.

A few hours later, the roof was as waterproof as it was going to get, and James was watching Mark play in the dirt under the kitchen window. James was trying to decide which chore to tackle next when he noticed that Mark had stopped playing and was staring off to the south. James turned and saw the two riders that had drawn Mark's attention away from his mud pies. James picked up his son and placed him inside the door of the cabin. Kaye started to protest about the dirty three-year-old on her clean floor until she saw James chamber a round into the rifle he kept above the mantel and place it just inside of the door jam. James pulled the door closed without latching it, and leaned up against the outside wall of the cabin to wait.

As the two men rode up, James recognized the one on the

right as Buckshot Jim Sloan, a hired gun of some reputation who got his name from the sawed off twelve gauge that he carried. Buckshot had aged quite a bit sense James had seen him last. He had the slight bulge around his midsection that comes with age and his hair had turned to salt and pepper. He did not know the kid with the fancy black hat and matching belt that was riding with Buckshot, but he had the cocky look of a boy who wanted to make a name for himself and that could mean trouble.

When the two men got close, Buckshot was the first to speak, "Howdy, we was wonderin' if you could tell us how far it is to Redemption from here?"

"It's about a days ride north, north-east of here. Depending on how big of a hurry you're in," James replied. The two men stayed close together making it easy for James to keep an eye on both of them.

"My name's Jim and this here is Jake. Recon we could water our horses before we move on?" They both kept their hands on their reins and away from their guns. James relaxed just a bit; if they were here for him they would have spread out and their hands would have been within striking range of their weapons.

"Sure, help yourself." The two men dismounted and led their horses to the watering trough by the well. James took a step forward to stay within comfortable conversation range, but still close enough to the house to dive for the rifle just inside the door. He noticed that the kid was wearing an expensive pair of boots, knee high shined leather with a pair of die on each side, the kind of flashy nonsense that most young hot heads thought was stylish.

After taking a drink from the well, Buckshot turned to James, "You know, you look a lot like a fella I used to know. He had that same kind of scar on his check."

James felt his stomach begin to tighten, "If we've ever met I can't say as I remember."

The conversation drew Jake's attention away from his own cup of water, "Yea. Didn't J.T. Winters have a scar like that? Seems as if I remember that from the stories I've heard."

James shifted his weight and got ready to dive for the door. He looked back over at Buckshot and tried one last time to defuse the situation. He gave a quick dismissive laugh, "Ha, J.T. Winters! Boy would my friends get a kick out of you thinking I was The Angel of Death. That might just be the best compliment I've ever got. No, the name's James Snow."

"Yea' Buckshot, what would the J.T. Winters be doing sod bustin'? Hell they say that Winters even stood down Wild Bill at the Alamo Saloon over in Abilene. The way that I heard it, Wild Bill was even afraid of The Angel of Death. So, what in the world would anybody that good be doin' in the middle of nowhere working a dirt farm?" Jake asked, completely dismissing the idea that this mere farmer could be the deadliest gun to have ever lived.

Jim looked disgustedly over at the kid, "Don't believe every story you hear. Winters and Hickcock are friends, that's why they never tried each other. Least they were friends."

"What do you mean *were* friends?" James asked. To the best of his knowledge Wild Bill was one of the best friends that he had ever known and one of the few men that he had ever really trusted. The two of them had shared everything from whiskey to women on several occasions.

"Hickcock's dead. Shot in the back while playin' poker up in Deadwood about three months ago," Buckshot replied as he watched James close for his reaction to the news.

As much as James wanted to ask if they had hung the man who had killed his friend, he held his ground. He knew that if he asked too many questions it would draw even more attention to his real identity. Instead, he tried to act as if he could care less, "Well I guess that Wild Bill deserved it. They say that he gunned down dozens men. I guess someone was bound the get him one day."

Satisfied with his response, Buckshot turned to his partner, "Well let's get goin'. We've wasted enough of this man's time. Much obliged for the water." The two men saddled up and rode off.

James watched the two ride away, then went back into the house and picked up the rifle. "What were those two men talking about? Did they really think that you were that killer?" Kaye asked. For the first time she really wanted to know the truth about James' past.

"They just had me confused with someone else, that's all," James said smiling at her lovingly. "It's nothing for you to worry your pretty little head about. They're gone and that's the end of it." James unloaded his rifle and placed it back over the mantel while he tried to decide if he was trying to convince his wife or himself that there was nothing to worry about.

***

When the two riders were out of ear shot of the farm, the kid started laughing, "I can't believe you thought that sod buster was J. T. Winters. What in the world would Winters be doin' on a farm?"

Buckshot Jim Sloan pulled up on the reins and looked the kid right in the eye, "That *was* Winters you little peckerwood. And if you live long enough, you'll learn that there are more important things in the world than just being fast. Maybe J. T. has finally figured that out."

The two men camped for the night without saying much

else to one another. Jake was still mad about the way Buckshot had talked to him after leaving Snow's farm. He was always talking down to Jake, treating him like a child, and never calling him Missouri Jake, just Jake or kid. One day he would show him that he was not a kid. Missouri Jake had killed thirteen men, not counting Indians and Mexicans, and he was getting tired of this old man, who had to rely on a scatter gun, treating him like an unwanted stepson. Jake knew that one day Buckshot would push him too far and Jake would show him once and for all just how deadly he could be.

It was about noon the next day when Buckshot Jim and Missouri Jake reached Redemption. Following the directions in the letter they carried, the two men turned due east until they reached the Black River. They followed the river north to the Hayes ranch. A very attractive young man with wavy blond hair about Jake's age rode up to meet them. "Can I help ya'll with something?" Buckshot noticed that he sat proud in his saddle, but without looking cocky like Jake.

"I'm Missouri Jake and this here is my partner, Buckshot Jim Sloan. Seems like I would be a little more friendly if I was you partner. Remember, you sent for us," Jake replied in his usual short-tempered way.

"I didn't write to nobody, my father did. My name's John Hayes. If you'll take a look over your right shoulder, that man covering you with a rifle from that rise is Drew Williams, our foreman. Now if you will follow me, I'll take you to my father."

Buckshot was impressed with the way that the young Hayes handled himself. Most kids his age would have bristled up and challenged Jake for talking to them that way. Instead, he merely showed that he had the upper hand and let it go at that. There was much to be said for self-restraint and Buckshot knew that Jake did not have an ounce of it in his entire body.

John led them to the main house were a large man in what appeared to be his early fifties with an abnormally large gray mustache stood waiting. "My name is Al Hayes. I take it by the fact that Drew didn't fill you full of holes that you are the two men I've been waiting for. Come on in the house and we'll talk business."

The two gunmen dismounted and followed Hayes through the front door and into his study. Buckshot noticed that the house did not have any resemblance of having a woman's touch. Given that he had already met Hayes' son, he assumed that Mrs. Hayes must have died some years back. The old man poured himself a drink and asked if the two gunmen would like one. Buckshot shook his head quickly for both of them. Missouri Jake shot him a glance, but held his tongue.

Hayes sat down behind the big cherry-wood desk; "Well let's get down to it then. I made a drive north from Texas about eight years ago and started this ranch. Things have been pretty good, fairly mild winters, not a lot of Indian trouble, and we've grown to be a good size outfit. Then, last year, Jack Coven brings a herd up and settles just north of me on the same river. Now, he has a pretty small outfit, but he's growing. My problem is if he gets too big or if we have a real dry summer, he could cut off all the water to my spread. So, I went to him and tried to get him to sign an agreement saying that he would guarantee not to interfere with the natural flow of the river, and if he does, I would be allowed certain financial reimbursements for whatever loses I might sustain. He says that he couldn't 'foresee all eventualities that may arise,' in that fancy educated voice of his and refuses to sign the damn thing. Now, what I need is for the two of you to either get him to sign the agreement, or, if he refuses, run him off his spread."

"How many men does this Coven have working for him?" Buckshot asked.

"About twenty or so, but most are just trail hands who stayed on for the steady work after the drive. He doesn't have any that I would consider to be gunmen. I figured with the extra fifteen men I have, and you two gentlemen to provide advice and intimidation, we should be able to convince Coven to see things my way." Hayes hesitated to receive a nod of understanding from each of his guests before he continued. "Now I figured that I would provide you with room and board, and an additional twenty-five dollars a week each. I trust that those arrangements will be suitable?" Hayes paused once more for each of the men to agree. "Good! Then John will show you to your bunkhouse."

The younger Hayes led the two gunslingers to their bunkhouse without saying a word to either of them. Once he was gone, Jake asked Buckshot, "You get the feelin' that the boy there don't like the idea of us helpin' as much as his old man does?"

Buckshot nodded slowly, then said, "Yea', I would reckon that his idea of how to handle the situation is a little different than his Pa's."

"Oh well, don't matter no how. This here job seems like a piece of cake if you ask me," Jake said as he threw his bedroll on to one of the empty bunks.

Buckshot rolled his eyes, "I don't remember askin'. And anyway, just how easy this job is would be up to this Coven fella, not you."

***

"I absolutely refuse to make it easy for that intolerable man to push me around," Jack Coven explained to his foreman and lead man. Nelson Bell and David Olenger had both worked for Coven for two years. They had helped him make all of the arrangements for his cattle drive north, lead the drive for him, and had run the ranch for the past year. They both wondered whether or not Coven could run the ranch for one day if they were not there to hold his hand.

Coven continued, "I did not close the store in Pennsylvania and move my wife and daughter all the way out to this Godforsaken land just so that uneducated barbarian could force me off my own land at gun point. Are you sure that he has resorted to requesting the services of hired killers?"

Olenger answered, "Yes, sir, Mr. Coven. One of our boys saw them skirt past town and followed them right up to the Hayes ranch. He said it was Buckshot Jim Sloan and Missouri Jake. Both of which are known gunslingers."

Coven got up from his chair and began to pace behind his desk. His fancy European style suite and waxed handlebar mustache only emphasized how out of place he was on the plains, "Hayes already has us out manned, and now he has added the services of these two professional killers. I am afraid that we may have no choice but to comply with his demands."

Bell saw this as the opportunity that he had been waiting for, "Sir, what if we fight fire with fire."

Coven stopped pacing. "What do you mean, Mr. Bell?"

"If Hayes wants to make this an all-out range war, then I say we do him one better. I've got a friend who knows how to get in touch with Monroe and the Eleven Disciples. I say that if Hayes wants to start a war, then we hire an army." Bell did not have to wait long for Coven's answer.

"Absolutely not! I will not have anything to do with that evil man or those mindless killers who follow him about. We will face our own adversities and we will find a gentile way to accomplish our goals or we will fail. I will not lower myself to such degradation. You are both excused gentlemen." Coven pointed to the door as if posing for a grand painting.

Bell and Olenger left the room without saying another word. Bell decided to be patient; he was sure another opportunity would present itself soon enough.

Once they were out of the room, Becky Coven burst in as if on cue. "What was that all about, Father?"

"Just business, my dear. Nothing that I would want my precious little girl to worry about," Coven responded. In his eyes, his daughter was still a child. He refused to notice what every other man on the ranch had, that his little girl was now quite grown and very attractive. Her small frame, long black hair, and sky blue eyes were enough to make her beautiful according to anyone's standards.

"Father, I have told you a million times, I do not like those two men. They are going to be trouble for you. I still do not see why you do not just sit down with Mr. Hayes and negotiate an appropriate agreement. John believes that he can get his father to listen—"

"I have told you not to converse with that boy!" her father interrupted. "I will not have my daughter associating with such riffraff. Do you understand me?"

"What is all this yelling about?" Olivia asked as she entered the room. Although she was now forty-five, it was obvious where Becky had gotten her striking looks.

"Your daughter refuses to understand that it is not her place to concern herself with the affairs of this ranch," Coven answered to his wife.

Becky stomped her foot on the hard wood floor, "I thought this ranch belonged to the entire family. I did not realize that it was a totalitarian dictatorship!" She then stormed from the room punctuating her exit by slamming the door.

"I swear, I will never understand that girl," Coven said. "Will you please have a talk with her about what the appropriate duties are for a young lady of her position?"

Olivia took her husband by the hand. "I will try, but you have to understand that we are not in Philadelphia. Becky is merely a product of her times and surroundings."

"That may be so," Coven sighed, "but that does not make it acceptable."

Olivia tried to make him understand. "For a woman to survive here, she has to be strong and not afraid to speak her mind."

Coven smiled. "Then I believe that our daughter will do more than survive. If this territory ever becomes a state, she just may find herself in the Governor's mansion one day, and I do not mean as the Governor's wife."

"Darling," Olivia started, "we also need to discuss your feelings toward John Hayes. I have seen the look in her eyes when she speaks of him."

Coven pulled his hand out of his wife's grasp. "It is not love if that is what you are implying. It is only a lack of suitable options."

"Whatever it happens to be, you would do well to be a little more understanding with her," his wife concluded.

CHAPTER 2

James corralled the last of his young horses and got his gear together. He knew that it would take him several days to break them all and prepare them for sale. He entered the small wooden corral with his rope and drew a bead on the first of the colts he would work with, a large paint out of his best mare. Once he had the young horse roped, he tied it to the center post and drove the remainder of the colts into the next corral.

Once Kaye saw that her husband's full attention was on the task at hand, she exited the house and quietly made her way across to the barn. She had always wondered about James' past, but deep down some part of her just did not want to know the truth. However, ever since those two men had ridden through the day before, her curiosity had consumed her. She had to find out once and for all exactly who the man she shared her bed with each night really was.

She started in the hayloft, but came up empty. She then moved to the area where James kept his tools. However, once again she found nothing. She was about to give up and go back to check on Mark when she noticed a saddle in the back corner of the barn that she had never seen before. It was very small and had a strip trough the middle of the seat where there was no leather at all. The strangest thing she noticed was that the saddle did not have a horn. Why would a man want a saddle that gave him no place to tie a rope off?

She lifted the odd saddle and found it to be very light. She then lifted the small saddle blanket that it was resting on and found that the blanket and saddle had been setting on a small wooden trunk. When she opened the lid, Kaye knew that she had found what she was looking for. Inside the trunk were two cap and ball pistols in black leather holsters. She removed one of the pistols and noticed that the front sight had been filed off. Again she was confused. Why would a man carry a gun that he could not aim? She slid the gun back into its holster and continued to search through the trunk.

She found a set of clothes that she had not seen James wear since they had first met on her father's farm. The shirt felt heavy, and when she investigated, she found that it had two derringer pistols placed in special pockets made into the shirt. One small pistol was in the right sleeve and the other was on the left rib-cage. She also found a very sharp knife on a strange figure-eight looking belt. When she examined the blade she found the words *Green River Knife Company* engraved into the steal. She was placing the knife back into the trunk when she heard someone behind her.

"What exactly are you looking for?" James asked.

Kaye's heart stopped. Not only was she startled by James' sudden appearance, but for the first time since she had known her husband she was afraid of him. "Answers," she replied, "I just thought it was time that I finally got some."

James lowered his head. "What do you want to know?" He was already ashamed of the answers he was about to give. He knew that once again he would have to lie, or at least give another series of half-truths, to try and appease his wife. He tried to decide if lying to her was wrong if he was truly doing it to protect her and Mark.

Some of Kaye's courage returned when she saw that her husband would not look her in the eye. Besides, this was her family and she deserved the truth. "What is all of this stuff?

What are you doing with it? I mean look at this saddle; I've never seen anything like it. I just want to know the truth." She sat back and waited for him to answer.

James wanted to tell her the truth, but he was afraid of how she would react to the knowledge that her husband was an infamous killer. He loved Kaye too much to hurt her in any way. James did not think that he could live with the fact that he had disappointed his wife.

"That's a Calvary saddle. It and the rest of that stuff is what's left of the gear I used in the war. I was in a special kind of unit. There were only a few of us and we had to travel light and fast. Our job was to disrupt the enemy supply lines and cause as much trouble as possible. That also meant doin' things that I am not very proud of, but it was no worse than what they did to our people." James hoped that the explanation would satisfy her, but he doubted that it would.

"What about what those men were saying the other day? Why would they think that you were that awful man?" Kaye tried to hold back the tears.

James walked over and took his wife in his arms. "I've told you, after the war I moved to Texas and started working cattle drives. I don't know what those two men were thinking. They just had me confused with someone else. I'm James Snow, not a killer."

Kaye did not ask any more questions. James hoped that this would be the last time that the subject would come up, but deep down he knew that J. T. Winters would haunt him for the rest of his life. Maybe it was time for him to move his family before his past caught up with him once again.

***

Olenger rode through the front gate of the Coven ranch

with his horse on a dead run. He galloped up to the main house, pulled back hard on the reigns, and dismounted before the pinto came to a full stop. Coven was sitting in a rocking chair on the front porch. "What appears to be the problem, Mr. Olenger?"

"Riders comin'. There's about thirty of them. Hayes is in the lead," Olenger answered. He tried to hide the nervousness he was feeling, but it came trough in his voice despite his best efforts.

"Well then, gather as many men as possible, and we shall see what we can do for our overzealous neighbor," Coven ordered in his best commanding voice.

Olenger sounded the dinner bell figuring that it was the best way to get everyone's attention. Men came running form all directions and gathered in front of the main house. By the time Hayes and his men arrived Coven had gathered eighteen men to face them.

Coven stepped out in front of his men flanked on his left by Olenger and on his right by Bell. Hayes brought his riders to a halt roughly ten passes in front of the defensive line that Coven's men had formed. Hayes advanced to meet Coven bringing Drew and Buckshot with him. Coven recognized Drew by his thin frame and sharp facial features and assumed that the older man with Hayes must be one of the gunfighters that he had hired. What worried him was that he did not know where Hayes' other hired gun was hiding.

Hayes broke the silence, "I think that it is time that we finalize our arrangements concerning the water rights we had discussed earlier."

Coven knew that if Hayes was willing to shot it out, he did not stand a chance. Hayes had him outnumbered by about twelve men, and he also had the two hired guns, only one of which was visible. The other had remained in the crowd, waiting to pounce without warning. "I believe that we have already discussed that matter in detail and you are fully aware of my position on the matter."

Hayes smiled in a way that reminded Coven of a predator showing his teeth just before it attacked. "Well, that was before I hired a few extra hands to help me out with some of my more pressing matters. I must admit that they are quite good at what they do. In fact, I believe that if we can't come to an agreement that I can feel comfortable with, I just may have to let these gentlemen give you a demonstration on just how effective they can be."

Coven felt his stomach begin to revolt against him. His head was spinning so fast that he did not even realize that an idea had come to him until he had already said it. "Very well, I will sign an agreement. However, you must give me two weeks to arrange for my lawyer to arrive from Philadelphia. I will not lend my signature to any legal document that has not been approved by my legal representative."

Hayes shifted in his saddle. He wanted to finish this now, but he also wanted all of his arrangements to appear as legal as possible. "Fine, but if your lawyer's not here in two weeks, I do not think you will like how the next round of negotiations will end."

Motioning for his men to follow, Hayes turned his horse and headed for his own ranch.

Buckshot asked Hayes, "Why didn't we just finish this while we had the chance? What in the world do you want to give him two more weeks for?"

Hayes grinned beneath his large mustache and dismissively answered, "I know Coven. In two weeks he will either sign the agreement or you will kill him. It's not like he has the guts to do anything about it. Besides, if any law enforcement types ever want to start asking questions, this makes it look like we tried to be reasonable, and it gives us time to come up with an excuse not to be reasonable."

John rode up beside his father and said, "Do you really think all of that strong arm talk was necessary?"

Hayes shot him a cold look and said, "Boy, last time I checked I was still in charge around here. Besides, where exactly were you back there? You should have been up front with me; instead you were nowhere to be found. If you're not enough of a man to face your enemies, I don't want people to know that you're my son." Hayes kicked his horse and trotted ahead of the rest of his men.

John turned to Buckshot looking unfazed by what his father had said. "I have to ride back now. I've got some business to take care of, but can you meet me and Drew later tonight behind the bunkhouse?"

Buckshot nodded to the younger Hayes, and the boy rode off. He knew that John was more of a man than most kids his age. He had to have been doing something important not to have been at his father's side. Maybe tonight he would get some answers about how things really worked around the Hayes ranch.

***

Coven and his men held their positions until Hayes and his entourage were out of sight. Bell turned to his boss and asked, "Are you really going to let them push us around like that? He shows up with a couple of hired guns and you're gunna to just fold?"

"I am not conceding to that blowhard. I am merely buying us time to think of a better option. There has to be a way to best that man." Coven removed his derby style hat and began to scratch his head in thought.

Bell saw the door of opportunity open once again. "Sir, Hayes just told you that he's willin' to kill to get what he wants. The only thing that he is goin' to understand is force. Two weeks is enough time to get Monroe and the Eleven here."

Coven looked up to the sky as if expecting the answer to fall from a cloud and hit him in the face. When it did not, he sighed. "Very well, but only tell them that we want to discuss a possible job. Do not promise them compensation for anything more than their travel expenses. Are we clear on that point, Mr. Bell?"

Bell lowered his head so that the bill of his hat would shield his smile from anyone who might be looking. He knew that Coven and most of the cowhands were too dumb to figure out why he was so pleased, but for now, he wanted to keep his little joke all to himself.

**

John Hayes rode toward Redemption until he was out of sight of his father and his men. He then circled back toward the north and stopped in a small grove of Oak trees just south of Coven's ranch. He dismounted his horse and sat under one of the larger trees to wait. Thirty minutes later, he heard a horse enter the grove from the north. John got to his feet and positioned himself behind the large tree to conceal his presence form the approaching rider.

Becky Coven rode into the small patch of trees and called out softly, "John, are you there?"

John stepped from his hiding place and replied, "Over here."

Becky jumped down from her bay and ran into John's waiting arms. "Oh John, I was so scared. I thought that your father was going to start shooting and—"

"Now, Now, everything is O.K." John tried to comfort her even though the same thought had haunted his mind at the time.

Becky pulled away from him saying, "No! Everything is not O.K. I heard father talking to Nelson Bell after your father's men rode away. They are sending for Monroe and the Eleven Disciples. I don't know who that is but they sound like more hired guns. This is all getting so crazy!"

John knew who Monroe and the Eleven Disciples were and it was far more ominous than Becky feared. They were the worse of the worse, hired killers who had no conscience and would kill anyone for the right price. This meant that Coven was willing to resort to all out war. "Hey, it's not that bad yet. We still have time to try and get our fathers to listen to reason."

Becky threw her arms around him again and said, "I'm just afraid that something bad will happen to you." She began to cry.

John leaned down and kissed her softly saying, "Nothing is going to happen to me. I love you too much to leave you here alone to marry one of those cowhands that work for your Pa." John wiped the tears from her eyes as she smiled up at him. The two of them held each other in the warm afternoon breeze and wished that time would stand still.

***

Buckshot Jim Sloan sat on a small hill overlooking James Snow's farm. When John had told him that Coven was sending for Monroe and his men, Buckshot knew that J.T. Winters was the only man who could help. The only question was if he would. Buckshot rode toward James' house not only hoping that he would agree, but also hoping that he would not be shot just for asking.

James met Buckshot at the front of the cabin, "You needin' more directions, Mister?"

Buckshot kept his hands in plain view while saying, "Nope, but we need to talk. The only gun I've got is the shotgun on my saddle and I'll leave it outside if you like."

James shook his head, "We got nothin' to talk about. Why don't you just be on your way?"

"Just hear me out. It has to do with Monroe." Buckshot hoped that would spark James' curiosity.

James stood staring at him for a long time and finally gave in "Come on in, but you best leave that scatter-gun where it is."

Buckshot dismounted and followed James into the house. When Kaye saw her husband enter the house with the stranger in tow she picked up Mark and went to the back room. James motioned for Buckshot to have a seat at the table then said, "Now, what's this all about?"

Buckshot took a seat. "I'm doin' some work for Al Hayes. He's got a spread outside of Redemption, and he's havin' some problems with one of his neighbors. Word is, his neighbor, Jack Coven, has hired Monroe to do some work for him. I just thought that you might want to know about it, with Redemption bein' so close to your little farm here."

James looked over Buckshot's shoulder to the door leading to the backroom. Buckshot glanced back over his shoulder in the same direction and realized James' wife had no idea about who her husband really was. James shifted uneasily in his chair. "How long before this Monroe guy gets here?"

"I reckon about two weeks or so," Buckshot answered. "Would you be interested in comin' up to Hayes' ranch and givin' us a hand with a few things?"

James looked shocked, as if the idea had not even entered his mind. "No. I don't do that kind of work. I used to know a guy who did, but he died about four years ago."

Buckshot nodded slowly. "In that case, you might want to think about stayin' out of town for a spell. It sure would be bad if someone was to get you and that fella that died confused."

James took a long hard look at his guest. "Does anyone else know about me or about what you came to talk to me about?"

"Not anybody that I can't control. I'll just tell 'em the guy I was lookin' for is dead, my memory must be slippin' in my old age." Buckshot stood up from his chair and said, "Well, I'll be gettin along. Sorry to have bothered you Mr. Snow."

James watched Buckshot leave. For the first time in four years his past had caught up with him. He wondered if the thirty miles between his farm and Redemption was enough to keep Monroe from finding him and his family. Hatred did not even come close to describing Monroe's feelings toward him. He believed that J.T. had betrayed him, and had vowed to see him die for that betrayal. If it had not been for blind luck and the kindness of a complete stranger he would have already been dead. James realized that he was involuntarily rubbing the scar around his neck when his wife entered the room.

***

Jack Coven's men dropped what they were doing and watched as Monroe and the Eleven Disciples rode up to the ranch. Monroe was in the lead. He was dressed in all black and was wearing a black flat-rimmed hat. He could have easily have been mistaken for a preacher if it was not for the two Navy Colts he was wearing. The eleven men with him were dressed like Monroe, except their cloths were brown instead of black. They all seemed to move as one, even when they dismounted they did so in unison.

Monroe walk to the porch were Coven stood waiting and said, "Are you Jack Coven?"

"I am. Thank you for coming on such short notice." Coven noticed that the expression on Monroe's face was impossible to read. He looked like a sculpture as if he was incapable of emotion.

"Shall we discuss your situation?" Monroe removed his hat and walked up onto the porch uninvited. Coven had to hurry to get to the door first. As the two entered, Coven noticed that Monroe's men stood as motionless as statues. They reminded him of the Royal Guards he had seen on his visit to London.

Coven lead Monroe to his study. Monroe's presence made Coven nervous, and the upside down cross he wore around his neck made him feel as if he had invited the devil into his home. Coven motioned for Monroe to sit but he refused, instead he stood motionless in the center of the room. Coven explained the situation with Hayes. While he spoke, Monroe did not say a word; Coven felt as if the tall thin man in black was looking right through him.

When Coven was finished, Monroe finally said, "Our services will be two-thousand a week, five-hundred for travel expenses, and we will required the use of a private bunkhouse."

Coven's mouth fell open, "That is rather expensive. I was hoping that we could negotiate..."

"Render unto Cesar the things which are Cesar's Mr. Coven, and in this situation I am Cesar." The expression on Monroe's face and the volume of his voice never changed, but the forcefulness with which he spoke made Coven fall back into his chair.

"Very well then. Mr. Bell will show you to your bunkhouse." As Monroe left the room, Coven felt as if he had no choice in the decision to hire the man and his followers.

When Monroe was gone Becky and Olivia entered the room. "Father, what have you done?" Becky asked.

"I have done what I must to protect my family and this

ranch," Coven responded. With Monroe gone, he once again felt as if he was in charge, and he was not going to have his actions questioned by his daughter.

Olivia stepped between her daughter and husband saying, "Jack, I agree with Becky. That man is a killer and he is not welcomed in this house."

Coven became furious. "This is my house! This is my ranch! I will decide who is welcomed and who is not. You will both tend to your own business and keep your noses out of mine!"

"Then that man and your greed will be the end of your house and your ranch! You cannot make a deal with the devil and think that you will not get burned!" Becky exclaimed.

"I will make a deal with whomever I please, and you will hold your tongue. So help me if it is the last thing I do I will teach you your place." Coven grabbed his hat and stomped toward the door.

"Mother, you have to speak with him. You cannot let him continue like this," Becky pleaded with Olivia.

"I know your father and once he has made a decision, nothing on the face of this earth can make him go back on that decision," Olivia said. Deep down she only hoped that he would live long enough to regret this one.

"He does have a way of making rash decisions and expecting everyone to just fall into line without asking questions," Becky said disgustedly.

"Now, dear," her mother began, "he only wants what is best for all of us. He just does not feel that John Hayes is your best choice for a husband."

Becky tried to look surprised when she said, "I have no idea what you are talking about!"

Olivia smiled and said, "Mothers have a way of knowing

things. Like how you have been sneaking off for secret rendez-vous down by the river."

Becky rolled her eyes then said, "And now I guess you are going to side with father and forbid me to see John?"

"No. I know that it would do no good to stand in your way," her mother explained. "I just ask that you wait for your father to come around. Do not fight him about John. If the boy is as wonderful as you believe, Jack will eventually see him for who he really is and not only for who his father is."

"That is if the men father hired does not kill him before he has a chance to see what a truly good man John is," Becky said.

"I am just as afraid of the evil that those men may cause as you are," her mother answered. "But, you have to have faith that God will protect us, and the ones we love, from the trials that lie ahead."

Becky gave Olivia a look of exasperation. "I do not think those men care at all about our loved ones, or even about God himself. I am afraid that they will be the end of us all."

CHAPTER 3

Missouri Jake entered the bunkhouse and found Buckshot cleaning his guns. "Word around the ranch is Monroe and his men are here. Did you have any luck with J.T.?"

Buckshot continued to work and answered the kid without looking up, "Nope. I reckon he's going to sit this one out."

"You know that we don't stand a chance without some help. Monroe and his men have us out-gunned. What are we goin' to do now?" Missouri Jake asked. He may have been cocky and over confidant, but he was smart enough to know when the odds were against him.

Buckshot looked up from his weapons disgustedly. "We are goin' to do what we were hired to do. If you ain't up to it, you can skin-out now."

Jake had the look of a child who had just been caught with its hand in the cookie jar. "I can handle it! I'm just sayin' it would be easier if we had another gun or two."

Buckshot finished putting his guns back together and stood facing Jake when he said, "Yea, well we'll see just what you can handle." Buckshot started out the door, then stopped and looked back over his shoulder. "A man in this business won't ever make a name for himself by only takin jobs when he knows he has the upper hand. You have to work a miracle or two along the way before most folks will take you serious." Buckshot then exited the bunkhouse leaving Missouri Jake alone to think things over.

Jake grabbed the chair he was standing next to and threw it across the room breaking it against the wall. How dare that washed up old man question his resolve. Jake knew that it was time to show Buckshot that he was not just some dumb kid with a gun. He had to do something that would prove once and for all that he did not need that old know-it-all to make all of his decisions for him and that he was able to take care of things himself.

Missouri Jake knew that he had learned all he was going to learn from the old man. Most of what he said was not worth remembering anyway. They had been hired to do a job, and all they had accomplished was wasting two weeks by sitting around and waiting for someone else to make the first move. Now they had lost their advantage. Monroe and his men were at Coven's place planning on how to kill them all. Jake knew that he would have to think of something. Buckshot was obviously content to just sit here and wait to die.

That was when the idea hit him. If he could get J.T. to join them after Buckshot had failed, the old man would have to respect him. Jake picked up his rifle and headed for the stable mumbling to himself, "I show that old son-of-a-bitch."

***

James Snow tied the five colts that he was taking to sell together on a lead line and gathered the rest of his gear. He put his bed role on the back of his saddle and placed the beef and corn-dodgers that Kaye had made for the trip into his saddlebags. He then went back into the house and pulled out the Peacemaker that he kept under the mattress. It was a good weapon, but he still preferred the cap and ball Navy Colts he kept in the barn. The Peacemaker just felt too light in his hand.

James walked into the kitchen and kissed his wife. "I'll be gone two days at the most. You finish going though the house and pickin' out what you want to carry with us. I'll load the wagon when I get back."

Kaye gave him a look of exasperation and said, "I still don't see why we have to leave. We've spent years making this place our home. I don't want to have to start all over again. Would you please just tell me what's going on? It has to do with that man that came back here the other day doesn't it? What did he tell you?"

James placed his hands lovingly on each side of her face as he said "I just think that it's best if we move on. Now I'm through talking about it. I want you to be ready to move out when I get back from selling those colts." James kissed her softly. "I love you. I just want what is best of you and Mark." He then walked out the door without looking back.

He knew that he would have to tell her the truth when he returned, but he wanted to enjoy just two more days of being James Snow. He only hoped that she would understand and forgive him. He also hoped that Stevens would give him a good price for his cattle, but there would be time to worry about that later. James saddled up and rode south toward Lakeside. He told himself that he could get a better price for the horses in Lakeside, but deep down he knew that he was afraid of Redemption.

Missouri Jake had been camped out watching J.T.'s ranch for two days. Now, he finally saw the opportunity he had been waiting for. He waited until J.T. had been gone for about an hour, then mounted his horse and rode down to the ranch.

***

Monroe sat motionless on his horse and waited for his scout to return. Five of his men sat behind him not moving or making a sound, four others were well out of sight serving as lookouts. When the scout returned, Monroe nodded in acknowledgement of his report and motioned for his men to move out. The four lookouts did not join the others. Instead, they rode out in a flanking maneuver two on the left flank and two on the right, just as they had done a countless number of times before.

Minutes later, the main body of Monroe's men topped the ridge and came into view of eight of Hayes' men working on a fence line just below them. Seeing that they had the approaching strangers outnumbered, Hayes' men stopped work and lined up to face the advancing riders. With their attention drawn to the seven approaching men, the fencing crew never saw Monroe's other four Disciples circle around behind them. Without saying a word Monroe's men opened fire. Three of Hayes' men were able to draw their weapons and squeeze off one shot each, but in the chaos of the moment their shots did not find targets.

When the smoke cleared, six of the eight were dead. The remaining two lay mortally wounded. Monroe dismounted and examined the two survivors. Once he had determined which of the two would live the longest, he fired a single shot into the forehead of the most seriously injured of the two men. He walked to each of the dead men, dipped the upside down cross he wore around his neck into their blood and placed a bloody brand onto each of their foreheads. Monroe then removed a canteen from his saddle and tossed it onto the ground beside the lone survivor who had suffered a serious stomach wound. "You should live until you are found. When your master arrives inform him that this is merely the beginning. It is appointed for man once to die and then the judgment. Tell Mr. Hayes his day of judgment has arrived," Monroe said, then turned, swung up into his saddle, and rode off with his men in tow.

The eleven followed their dark leader back to the Coven Ranch. Once there, the men dismounted and cared for their horses.

Jack Coven marched up to Monroe with Bell and Olenger following close behind. "Where have you been Mr. Monroe?"

"I have been doing what you hired me to do," Monroe answered without looking up from the hove he was examining.

"What exactly does that mean, Mr. Monroe?" Coven asked. His impatience was beginning to show in his voice.

Monroe released the hove and turned slowly to Coven. "I was increasing our numerical advantage. The two professional gunmen were not among them; however seven of Hayes' men have gone to face their maker. With an eighth soon to follow."

Coven's mouth fell open. "I did not authorize any such action! I hired you and your men to intimidate Hayes not to start a war!"

"You hired me to settle your little water dispute. If there is no one left to oppose you, then you have won." Monroe turned on his heels and entered the bunkhouse. His men looked at Coven as if daring him to speak again.

Coven half-furious and half-terrified stomped off to the main house mumbling to himself. Convinced that there would be no further confrontations, Monroe's men filed into the bunkhouse.

Bell smiled and began to chuckle softly. Olenger asked him, "What's so funny?"

Bell smiled at his friend and said, "This is perfect. That lunatic is makin' it too easy."

"Are you goin' let me in on your joke, or are you goin to just keep grinnin' like a weasel in the hen house?" Olenger asked.

Bell stopped smiling. "That know-it-all Coven couldn't run this place for a day if it weren't for us. Hell, he couldn't find his own ass if he used both hands. Now all we have to do is write the Marshal. He shows up, arrests Coven for hirin' Monroe and his pack of killers, we get the reward for those twelve, and we end up with the ranch to boot." Bell's smile returned, this time looking slightly more devious than before.

Olenger could not believe what he was hearing. Could Bell really be that underhanded? He had known him for several years and he had always been the kind of person that you could not trust in a card game, but this plan of his was pure evil. Olenger wondered if he could even call this man his friend now that he knew Bell was capable of such deviousness.

He knew that he had to try and bring Bell back to his senses. Olenger began to shake his head while saying, "You'll never get away with it. Let's say you do get by with it without Monroe killin' you. That still don't solve the problem of Hayes. Those murderers just started a war. With them in jail, how are you goin' to take on those hired guns Hayes has?" Olenger hoped that pointing out this flaw in his plan would discourage his friend from following through with the scam.

Bell's smile quickly faded. "You know, you're right." He rubbed his chin in deep thought. "I've got it. We just hold our cards for a while. We don't write the Marshal until Monroe and his men have taken care of Hayes for us. That way we get twice the pot. That's a ranch for both of us."

Olenger had never seen this side of his friend, and he did not like it. "It'll never work. You won't get away with it. Besides, Coven pays you a fare wage, why do you want to bushwhack him?"

Olenger could see the hatred building in Bell's eyes as he answered, "Cause we do all the work and that fancy pants sits on his ass and just gets richer. And what do you think will happen when Coven dies? We won't get a red cent, that's what'll happen. He'll leave it all to that smart-ass girl of his, and that's just half of it. Little Miss Loudmouth has been sneakin' off to see John Hayes. If we don't take what we deserve now, it will all end up goin' to those two kids, and I'll be damned if they get what I've worked to build."

Olenger shook his head and said, "I won't be a part of it. If you can live with swindling a man out of his land, that's fine, but I can't." Olenger turned his back to Bell and walked off toward the barn.

Bell called out to him as he walked away, "You keep you're mouth shut! If you don't want in that's fine, but don't you ruin this for me."

Olenger answered with a dismissive wave over his shoulder.

Bell was surprised that Olenger did not want a cut of the action. They had ridden together for years and he thought that he could rely on him to back his play. At least now he knew that he could not be trusted. If push came to shove Bell knew that he would have to kill Olenger. He had come too far to let anyone stand in his way.

***

James Snow could finally see his spread in the distance. He had gotten a good price for his colts in Lakeside, and now he was trying to decide what he would tell Kaye about his past. He had a feeling that she already knew the truth, but he was worried about how she would react when hearing it from him. He loved her and Mark dearly. The last thing he wanted to do was to hurt either of them. He had decided that even though he was going to tell Kaye everything, he did not want Mark to know who or what his father used to be. He did not want his son to have to pay for the sins of his father.

As James got closer, he could see that something was not right. There was no movement coming from the farm, and there was something out of place. As he got closer he could see that there was something hanging from the side of the barn. He kicked his horse up to a trot, then to a full gallop. He began to get sick at his stomach. James started to pray that he was wrong about what he thought he was seeing. He jumped off of his horse before it came to a stop, and fell to his knees. His chin hung down to his chest and for the first time since he was a small boy, he began to weep.

He slowly raised his head and through his tear filled eyes he looked at the two naked bodies hanging crucifixion style on the side of the barn. Between them a large upside down cross was branded into the rough wood slabs. As quickly as the tears had come, they stopped. His grief and terror was immediately replaced with blind rage. Not only toward Monroe for taking the only two people he had ever loved, but also toward himself. This was his fault. His wife and son were dead because he had run from his past instead of standing and facing it like a man.

James got to his feet, and on shacking legs, removed the bodies of Kaye and Mark from the side of the barn. He went down by the creek to Kaye's private place where she went to think and pray, and there he dug two graves side by side. He placed the bodies into the graves and slowly covered them with dirt. He fell to his knees between the two fresh mounds. James reached out and placed a hand on each of them. After what seemed like and hours, he got to his feet and walked into the creek. He entered the creek and washed off the dirt and sweat from burying his family; he washed off James Snow.

.

J.T. walked up to the corral and removed the boards, which served as an entrance and then drove all the horses out of the pen. Next, he opened the main gate. There were no cows in site, but he knew that they would find their way to the opening come feeding time. J.T. then went into the cabin to retrieve his rifle before finally going to the barn.

He led his horse down to the graves of his wife and son.

J.T. removed the bandana that he had used to hide the scar on his neck and placed it on his wife's grave, "Don't worry my love, I'll be with you soon. Right after I send Monroe to where he belongs, straight to Hell." J.T. mounted his horse and rode for Hayes' Ranch.

J.T. ignored the lookout that had spotted him at Hayes' property line. He continued at a steady pace toward the group of building in the distance. As J.T. rode up to the main house, men came from all directions and surrounded him as he sat in his saddle just in front of the porch. There was something about the stranger in the faded Calvary hat and long duster that brought a twinge of fear to them all.

Al Hayes walked out onto the porch holding a shotgun. "Can I help you partner?"

J.T. looked up from under the brim of his hat and said, "Are you Hayes?" He waited for the older man to answer.

"That depends on who's askin'," Hayes responded.

J.T. simply spat on the ground in response. "I've come to tell you that I'm goin' to kill Monroe, and I don't want your men gettin in the way," He was surprised when Hayes began to laugh.

"I've got enough trouble around here without wastin' time talkin' to some two-bit bounty hunter out for a fast buck. If you want Monroe, then you'll just have to beat us to him. Now get out of here," said Hayes, and then turned to go back into the house.

Buckshot was leaned up against the corner of the house and decided that he had better speak up before things got ugly. "I wouldn't turn my back on the Angel of Death if I were you." Hayes stopped in his tracks, a cold chill ran up his back, and he turned slowly and looked over toward Buckshot. Sloan continued, "Al Hayes, I would like for you to meet the fastest gun that ever lived, Mr. J.T. Winters.

Hayes turned and faced J.T. careful not to point the shotgun he was holding anywhere near the stranger. "Are you really the Angle of Death?"

J.T. just looked right through him.

"What do you want with Monroe?" Hayes asked.

"What I want with Monroe is my business," J.T. responded.

Hayes nodded, "If you need a place to stay you can bunk up over there. Monroe and his men have already killed eight of my ranch hands. I'm goin' to the Sheriff in the mornin' to see if he will do anything about it. I doubt that he will, but you're welcome to come along if you want."

J.T. had nowhere else to stay, so without saying a word, he turned his horse and rode in the direction of the bunkhouse. Once Hayes had entered the house and the crowd of onlookers went back to what they had been doing before J.T. arrived, Buckshot went to find Missouri Jake. He found him behind the barn with a smug look on his face. "What the hell did you do?" Buckshot demanded.

"I did what you couldn't. I went and got the help we needed," Jake replied, obviously pleased with himself.

Buckshot could not believe how dumb this kid really was. "I'll tell you what you've done. You've just signed your own death warrant if he ever finds out what really happened."

Jake laughed. "Then I don't see any reason why he should ever find out."

Buckshot stuck his finger in the youngster's face. "You better hope that he don't. Your playin' with a fire that you can't control boy."

Jake shoved his finger away and said, "Watch who you're threatening old man. You're just pissed I found a way to get the help we needed when you couldn't. I ain't sacred of some washed up sodbuster. I can handle him."

Buckshot shook his head and said, "You have no idea how good he is do you? I promised your Pa I'd look after you, so I won't tell J.T. what you've done. But once were finished with this here job, you're on you own." Then Buckshot turned and walked away.

"Oh yeah," Jake called after him. "Well that's fine with me. I don't need you no how!"

***

Becky was already in the grove of trees when John rode up. She ran over and placed both hands on his knee and asked, "What has happened?"

John pushed her hands away and dismounted. "Your father, that's what happened."

Becky could see that he was very upset. "It's those horrible men; they have done something haven't they?"

John calmed down when he saw how scared she was. "Yea, they rode over to our place and killed eight of our men. They just shot them down like animals. They left one man alive to give a warning to my father, but he died an hour after we found him. Becky, tell me your father didn't tell them to do that. He wouldn't order them to shoot men down like that would he?"

Becky shook her head vigorously. "No! He told me he hired them just to keep the men that your father hired from running us off our land." Becky threw her arms around John and laid her head on his shoulder. "What are we going to do? What if they hurt your father? What if they come after you next? John we have to do something."

John returned her embrace. "I know. But for now I think that it's too dangerous for us to see each other again for a while. We're goin' to the Sheriff tomorrow to see if he can help."

Becky pulled back and looked John in the eye. "I wouldn't

count on it. I heard my father tell Nelson Bell that they didn't have to worry about the Sheriff getting involved."

John leaned down and kissed her. "I don't know what will happen, but whatever does, I want you to know that I love you."

Becky pulled away from him, "You cannot tell me that you do not want to see me again and then say that you love me!"

John tried to explain. "It's just till things blow over. I'm not saying that I never want to see you again. All I'm saying is that with Monroe and his men at your father's ranch, what would happen if they followed you here?"

"But I was careful," she answered. "I made sure no one saw me leave."

"It doesn't matter how careful you are. If those men find out about us they could use you to get at me, and I couldn't stand the thought of you being hurt like that." John then turned and walked toward his horse. "It won't be forever, just until all of this is settled." John swung up onto his saddle and looked back at Becky to see her unbuttoning her dress.

John's eyes widened. "Becky, what are you doing?"

She looked up at him lovingly. "This may be the last time we see each other, and..." her voice softened toward the end and she could not find the words to express what she was feeling.

John understood her meaning all too well. He stepped down out off his horse and took her in his arms. They lay down together in the grass by the river.

CHAPTER 4

J.T. tossed and turned all night while James Snow and J.T. Winters fought over what to do next. J.T. wanted to track down Monroe and kill him as soon as possible, but years of listening to Kaye's advice had him wondering if he should. Buckshot had also given a very convincing argument for going to the Sheriff after he had returned to the bunkhouse. J.T. fell asleep still not knowing what he would do the next day. At sometime during the night, J.T. dreamed of Kaye, and when he woke the next morning he decided to try it her way.

J.T. and Buckshot saddled their horses and met Hayes, his son, and Drew Williams in front of the main house. J.T. explained to Hayes that it was best if his real name was not used, and it was decided that his alias of James Snow would be the name given to the Sheriff.

As the group headed for town, J.T. noticed that John Hayes was in an unusually good mood considering the circumstances. The younger Hayes was humming to himself and smiling like all in the world was wonderful. J.T. chalked it up to the ignorance of youth and thought little else about it. J.T. then rode up to the elder Hayes and said, "I'm sorry about your men, but I want you to know that if the Sheriff doesn't want to help, Monroe is mine."

Hayes agreed and replied, "You probably have the best chance of any of us at actually killin' him. Sloan there is good, but I think he's past his prime. I just don't know about that kid, Jake. He didn't even want to ride with us when he heard you were comin' along. But, you may have a hard time of convincing Drew that you have first call on Monroe. Four of my men that were killed were kin of his, and he's determined to get even."

J.T. looked back over his shoulder at Drew. He recognized the look of determination on ranch foreman's face. It was the look of a man hungry for vengeance. J.T. thought that the same look was probably on his own face. "I'll worry about that when the time comes. But in the meantime I want you to know that I don't care about what problems you have with Coven. I ain't asked you for a dime. I don't work for you; I just want Monroe."

As the group entered town, Drew told Hayes that he was going to the telegraph office to send word to his family about his relatives that had been killed by Monroe and his men. The four remaining members of the party rode up to the front of the jail.

A young deputy in what appeared to be his early twenties sat in a wooden chair out front. "You fellas need some help?" The deputy had a cocky way about him that reminded J.T. of the young gun hand that traveled with Buckshot.

"Were looking for Sheriff Mossman," Hayes answered.

"What do you want to see him about?" the deputy responded. "He's real busy."

The four men dismounted, and Hayes walked up onto the planked sidewalk. "I'm sure he is, but what business I have with him is between me and him and doesn't involve you."

"Come on in Mr. Hayes," a voice called from inside of the jail. The four men walked in with the young deputy in tow. "You'll have to forgive my younger brother," Sheriff Steve Mossman said from behind his desk. "He's a little overzealous with his new position." The younger Mossman looked irritated at his older brother's rebuke.

"We are here to report a series of murders," Hayes explained. He then proceeded to inform the Sheriff of all the details, including the murder of J.T.'s family. Of course, he failed to mention his hiring of Buckshot Sloan and Missouri Jake, or his initial attempt to intimidate Coven.

The Sheriff listened to the entire story before he responded, "Mr. Hayes, I am sorry for your loss, and the same goes for you Mr. Snow. However, my job is to uphold the law here in Redemption. Your land and especially that of Mr. Snow's is well outside of my jurisdiction. In addition, I know all about your strong-arm tactics in relation to Mr. Coven's water rights. I'm sorry, but there is nothing that I can do for you."

Hayes looked as if he had been slapped in the face when he said, "I should have known you would be no help. How much did Coven pay you to stay out of it?"

Mossman shrugged then said, "As I said, there is nothing I can do for you. By the way, I would like to know if Mr. Snow's ranch is a day's ride south of here, how exactly was Monroe and his men able to kill your men and his family on the same day?"

J.T. felt as if the world was spinning around him. How had he not seen this before? It was impossible for Monroe to have killed his wife and son. The man who had lived long enough to tell Hayes what had happened had said that there were twelve men who had attacked them. J.T. walked out into the street to clear his head.

When the others joined him, J.T. turned on Buckshot. "You were the only one who knew where I was," the anger building in his voice, "I'll give you one chance to tell me the truth."

Buckshot lowered his eyes. "J.T., it wasn't me. It was the kid. I didn't know what he was goin' to do. You have to believe me." Buckshot continued to explain, but J.T. did not hear another word. He could only hear the sound of his heart pounding in his ears.

The rage continued to build in J.T. His hand began to move as if he had no control over his own body. Before J.T. even knew what was happening, he reached behind his head and had pulled his knife from its scabbard that was held in place by the figure eight belt, which concealed the knife in the middle of his back. J.T. brought the knife around in one quick fluid motion and slashed Buckshot's throat. A woman walking down the street screamed like a banshee at the sight of Buckshot clasping the open wound with both hands trying in vain to stop the blood from gushing from his body. A moment later he fell to the street motionless. The blow had been so severe that it had almost de-capitated the old gunman.

The young deputy came bounding through the jailhouse door with his gun drawn in response to the woman's scream. In-stinct took control of J.T. when he saw the brandished weapon. J.T. dropped his knife and made a half turn to his left, drew both of his pistols, and fired them both at the same time. The force of both rounds striking the deputy in the chest sent his body flying back through the jailhouse door, were it collided with the Sheriff who was rushing to find out what was going on in his quiet little town.

Mossman found himself on the floor of the jail with the dead body of his younger brother lying on top of him. He rolled the lifeless corpse to the side and exited the jail, firing at the men who he thought had just killed his brother. His first shot struck Al Hayes in the stomach and his second hit the dirt just in front of John Hayes causing him to jump back as if a snake had struck at him. Mossman never fired a third round. The Navy Colt that J.T. was holding in his left hand barked fire and smoke once again and the bullet struck Mossman in the right elbow. The force of the impact threw the Sheriff hard to his left, causing him to strike his head on the door jam and knocking him un-conscious.

J.T. stood in the street with both guns drawn. When he was convinced that the fight was over, he holstered the weapons and picked up his knife. He looked over at John. The young Hayes had a look of horror on his face. The kid had probably never seen a killing before, much less two men killed and two seriously wounded in a matter of seconds. J.T. decided that it would be best to skin out before some of the more adventurous townspeople decided to avenge their Sheriff and his brother. He mounted his horse and headed south for his farm. On the way out of town he passed Drew running toward the sound of the fight. Drew stopped and watched J.T. pass, then ran down the street to check on his friends.

***

Once Bell, Olenger, and Monroe were gathered in his office, Coven began to speak, "Gentlemen, I have some rather disturbing news. Sheriff Mossman and his deputy were brutally attacked in town today. Our good Sheriff will live, however, Dr. White has informed me that he has a serious head wound and the Doctor had to remove his right arm at the elbow. Unfortunately, the Sheriff's younger brother was killed instantly. He suffered two gunshot wounds to the chest at close range. Furthermore, Mr. Al Hayes received a gunshot wound to the stomach and it is doubtful that he will live through the night. Also killed was one of Mr. Hayes' hired guns. He apparently had his throat slashed and died rather quickly."

"Why would Hayes and his men attack the Sheriff?" Olenger asked.

"They did not accost the Sheriff directly," Coven responded. "It appears that the confrontation began when a man with Mr. Hayes' party cut the throat of the hired killer. There are conflicting stories on what exactly happened next, but it would appear that the same unidentified man killed the deputy and wounded the Sheriff. It seems that Mr. Hayes was merely caught in the crossfire."

Monroe interrupted, "What do you know about the 'unidentified' man?"

"Only that he killed the hired gun with a knife that was concealed under his coat, I believe they said it was carried in the middle of his back, and that he carried two Navy Colt revolvers. Rather primitive if you ask me, but he apparently is rather skilled with them," Coven responded.

For the first time since he had met Monroe, Coven saw a glimpse of emotion on his face. He was not sure if it was excitement or fear. Monroe moved closer to Coven and said, "Did this man have scars on both his check and his neck?"

Coven was surprised, "Why, yes. I believe they said he did. Do you know who he is?"

Monroe did not answer. He simply turned and exited the room

Coven shrugged and turned his attention back to his men. "This is rather unfortunate. I am afraid that the Marshal will be summoned to look into this. The Sheriff had been persuaded to see things our way, but the Marshal is not as fiscal minded as Mr. Mossman."

"What's your next move?" Bell asked.

"To end this before the Marshal arrives," Coven answered. "Tomorrow we will inform Mr. Monroe that with Al Hayes dead, his services are no longer needed. Then we will contact John Hayes and propose a reasonable conclusion to this mess. By the time the Marshal reaches Redemption, this will all just be a bad memory."

Bell kept a solemn face while talking with Coven, but on the inside he was jumping with joy. Hayes was dying, Coven was getting rid of Monroe, and the Marshal would arrive in about a week. Everything was working out even better than he had planed.

***

Later that evening, John Hayes brought his father's body back to the ranch. He was still in shock over what had happened earlier that day in town. He had heard stories of gunfights, and like most young men, the idea had always fascinated him. Now having seen one first hand, and lost his father in the process, he hoped never to see another.

As he pulled the borrowed buckboard up to the house, the ranch hands gathered to hear what had happened. John relayed the story of the day's events without looking directly at anyone. No one could believe that J.T. had been as fast as John said. The way that he told the story made the gunslinger sound almost superhuman.

Missouri Jake became increasingly uncomfortable. "Why did Winters kill Buckshot?"

John looked over at Jake. "I don't know for sure. It had something to do with how his family died. I really didn't hear all that was said."

Jake slowly worked his way through the gathered crowd. Without drawing attention to himself, he entered the barn, saddled his horse, and rode west. Drew was the only one to notice Jake's exit. Suddenly, everything began to come together. The kid had killed J.T.'s family, not Monroe. Buckshot had known the truth, and that was why J.T. had killed him.

Drew walked over to John and said, "I know there is a lot to be done, but I have something I need to do. Your father was like a father to me too, but I have to go. Can you take care of things here?"

John nodded in response. Drew was not sure if the kid had understood him or not, but it was the answer he had hoped for. He saddled his horse and rode back to town to try and pick up J.T.'s trail.

***

Missouri Jake rode west at a steady pace. He had used the fact that everyone's attention had been drawn to the story of how Al Hayes had been killed to make his exit. He knew that there was no need to hurry, even if J.T. came after him, Jake would have at least a full day's head start. In addition, J.T. would have no idea which direction he had gone.

Jake did not know where he was going, but it really did not matter. With Buckshot dead, he had no connections with anyone. He had been riding with his father's old partner for a year, every since his old man had been hanged in Dodge City. His father had asked Buckshot to look after Jake the night before he was killed. Of course, neither of them had stopped to ask Jake what he thought of the arrangement.

Buckshot never really wanted Jake tagging along, but he felt that he had to keep his word. Jake never liked the old man either, but he had not had any other options at the time. Now Buckshot was dead because he could not keep his big mouth shut, and for the first time in his life, Jake was on his own. The thought of not having to answer to anyone made him smile. He had waited seventeen years for this day.

Now he was free to make a name for himself. He could call his own shots and work for whomever he pleased without anyone trying to tell him what to do. And, if J.T. Winters decided to come looking for trouble, then the name Missouri Jake would go down in history as the man who finally killed the Angel of Death. Jake smiled again. Now that would be something to be proud of.

CHAPTER 5

J.T. rode up to the small hill overlooking his farm. He knew that if Monroe learned where the ranch was that it would be the first place that he would look for him, but J.T. had nowhere else to go. It was hard to believe that just two days ago he had been James Snow with a loving wife and son. Now he was J.T. Winters once again, and he already had blood on his hands. How was it possible for him to fall back into a life so quickly that he had walked away from so many years ago?

He looked down by the creek and could just make out the small mounds of his family's fresh graves by the light of the moon. J.T. had never felt regret for killing before. However, this time it was different. Buckshot had known who had really killed his family, but he had not played a part in it, in fact he had tried to warn him. Did he deserve to die just for knowing about the murders? Buckshot must have been the one who told the Missouri Jake that James was actually J.T. Winters, but J.T. should have packed his family and moved as soon as Buckshot told him about Monroe. Instead, he had waited until after he had made some money off his colts. Were Kaye and Mark dead because he had been greedy?

And what about the Sheriff and his brother? They were simply doing their job, now the deputy was dead and Mossman, if he was not dead, would never be the same again. They certainly did not deserve what had happened to them. Now, the best that J.T. could hope for was that a Marshal would be looking for him, but if his luck held to its usual form, he would have a grieving brother out for revenge on his trail.

Furthermore, J.T. had sided with Hayes and his men, but with Al Hayes dead because of J.T.'s killing spree, it was a good bet that no one at the Hayes ranch would lose a minute's sleep if J.T. met an early demise. Now to top things off, Monroe had to know that he was here and would undoubtedly be gunning for him.

What could he do now? He would have to go after Missouri Jake. J.T. would ride to the Hayes ranch in the morning and kill him. Even if he ran, he should not be hard to find with his fancy hat and idiotic looking boots. There were two things that you could always count on when tracking down that type of trash: they would always be too yellow to stand and face you and were too dumb to hide. They would just run.

J.T. had been so deep in thought that he had not noticed the rider approach his ranch until he had dismounted and walked into the house. J.T. pulled his rifle from the scabbard on his saddle and slowly began to make his way down to the house. The intruder had exited the house and entered the barn by the time J.T. moved into position and lowered his rifle on the barn door. When the man came back through the door J.T. had him dead to rights.

"Hold it right there!" J.T. announced firmly. "What the hell do you want?"

The man's hands immediately came up in front of him and away from his guns. "It's Drew Williams. I just came to talk to you. I'm not lookin' for any trouble."

J.T. stood up keeping his rifle aimed at Drew's chest. "We've got nothin' to talk about. How many men do you have with you?"

"It's just me," Drew responded, "no one else even knows that I'm here. I just came to tell you if you're goin' after Monroe, I want to help."

J.T. lowered his rifle to his hip, but kept it pointed in Drew's direction. "What do you want Monroe for?"

Drew hooked his thumbs behind his belt buckle so that he looked more natural, but his hands were still away from his guns. "Four of the men that Monroe killed at our ranch were my cousins. I mean to see him die for it."

J.T. remembered Hayes telling him that some of the men that were on the fencing crew that were gunned down were kin of Drew's, so his story made sense. "Why should I let you help?"

"Two against twelve ain't good odds, but it's a sight better than you goin' at it alone," Drew answered.

J.T. lowered his rifle and stood looking at Drew. He hated to admit it, but Drew had a good point. He had not given any thought to if he was going after Monroe or not. J.T. knew that he was going to hunt down the kid who had killed his family. However, he had not given any thought about what to do about Monroe. He had managed to avoid him and his men for several years, but now they were back on his trail. If he did not end this while he had the chance, tracking Missouri Jake would be even harder with someone trailing him.

"O.K., get your horse and follow me. It's too dangerous to stay down here at the house." J.T. then turned and began walking back up the hill.

Drew followed J.T. to the top of the rise overlooking the farm were he unsaddled his horse. It was only then that he realized how lucky he had been. J.T. could have shot him on site without asking any questions. He had heard stories about how ruthless the Angel of Death had been in the range wars in Texas. After hearing about the killings in Redemption, Drew believed that most of the stories he had heard were probably true, but if that was the case, why had J.T. not shot him when he exited to barn? Drew looked over and saw J.T. staring down at the farm, lost in thought.

The quiet began to make Drew uncomfortable so he decided to break the silence, "What do you know about Monroe?"

J.T. continued to stare down at the farm and answered without looking up, "More than I want to know. We rode together during the war until we had a difference of opinion, and he swore to see me dead for crossin' him."

Drew smiled and said, "That must have been some difference of opinion. I've had my share of arguments with folks in the past, but can't say that I ever wanted to kill someone over not seein' things my way."

"You're not Monroe," J.T. responded. "Besides, I didn't disagree with his opinion, I disagreed with his crusade."

J.T. had not thought of the old days in years, and he could not remember a time when he had ever told anyone the entire story. However, for some reason he felt the need to tell it now. Did he want Drew to know about all the details of his life? No, he really did not care if Drew knew why Monroe wanted him dead or not. Maybe deep down he needed to remind himself of how he had got to this point. Was there a good reason why a boy from Northwest Alabama had grown up to be a lethal killer?

J.T. walked over to where Drew sat on the ground leaned back against his saddle. J.T. adjusted his own saddle to make himself a seat and then settled in and started to tell the story. He simply stared at the ground and began to recite the events of his life during the war as if he was replaying it all in his mind.

"I grew up in Winston County, Alabama, up close to the Mississippi line. When the war started, most of the people in that area wanted nothin' to do with it. The way we saw things, it was a rich mans war. The whole fight over slaves and state rights had nothin' to do with the small farmers in our part of the country. Hell, if you had enough money and land you didn't even have to fight, you could hire someone to go for you. Not long after Alabama seceded from the Union we had a meetin' at Looney's Tavern to decide what to do. Nobody wanted to fight a rich man's war for 'em, but nobody wanted to fight their neighbors neither. So we just decided to stay out of the whole thing. Let the world go crazy if it wanted to, we would just sit there and wait on things to sort themselves out."

J.T. never looked at Drew during the story; he just stared at the ground and recited the story as if he had shared it with a thousand people before. Drew had no idea that he was the first person to ever hear the whole story of how the legend of J.T. Winters was born. J.T. continued, "We thought stayin' out of things was a good idea, but we had no way of knowin' that the rest of the state would label us traitors for it. They started callin' us the 'Free State of Winston,' and took to the idea that if we weren't with them then we had to be against them. They started sendin' riders in to kidnap boys old enough to fight. They would take them to Jasper and put 'em in a cell. They had three days to decide to join the Confederate Army. If they refused they were shot in the back of the head."

Drew was amazed. He had never heard of the "Free State of Winston" or any of the things J.T. was talking about. He found it hard to believe that people were kidnapped and shot for trying to mind their own business. But, he had heard of the problems in Kansas and Missouri during that time, so the story was much easier for him to believe than it would have been before the war.

Drew realized that J.T. had still been telling his story while he had been lost in thought, "... when that didn't have the result, they were lookin' for, they started torturin' members of your family to get at you."

Drew noticed that the tone in J.T.'s voice changed. He seemed very distant now, almost as if part of him was back in the time he was speaking of, and the rest of him was here relaying what it was seeing.

"That's when they got my brother, Jimmy. They tied him to a tree and did things to him that would make the devil lose his supper. So I joined up with Monroe. He had seen enough killin' and was lookin' for revenge after the same bunch killed his younger brother too. Monroe was the preacher in the small church just outside of Double Springs, so people followed him. He was a community leader, their Shepard. Ten boys from Winston county, includin' me, and two brothers from Pikeville over in Marion county, joined up with Monroe, and we all set out to make things right. We tracked down the boys from Jasper that had be doin' the torturin' and killin'. The funny thing is after we killed 'em we didn't feel any better. We still wanted more. It was funny how killin' never filled the hole you had inside. Anyway, we started goin' after others, even small detachments of Confederates in the area."

Drew noticed that J.T. now held a strange, almost evil tone. He noticed that his eyes even seemed to turn red and dark. It was almost as if he was possessed by a demon. He wondered if that was how he had gotten the name The Angel of Death.

J.T. continued with what almost sounded like a sense of pride in his voice, "We were good at our job, too. We lost a man every now and then, but there was always someone willin' to take his place. Monroe always wanted twelve, no more no less. He started to think of himself as the Messiah sent to save his people from the evil surroundin' 'em, and we were his twelve apostles, sworn to follow our leader and to spread his word of death and destruction. Every time the Reb's sent people in to kidnap or harass someone, we would hunt them down and make them pay. The way we treated the ones we caught wasn't alot different from what they were doin' to our folks. The difference was they deserved everything they got.

"When the Union captured Florence, we thought that the tide had finally turned in our favor. We even worked with a Union Calvary outfit to raid Jasper and free some of the folks they were holdin' there. But the Calvary decided that they did not need our help and told us to leave the fightin' to them. Their officers were afraid that some of our tactics was goin' to get them in trouble with the higher ups. They had a problem with the way we didn't take prisoners, and they really got mad when we set fire to the town. Monroe refused to hand over our weapons and we took to the hills again, but now we were avoidin' both sides. One of the boys decided that he had had enough and let out. Monroe tracked him down and hung him for it.

"That's when Monroe started to change. Just goin' after the Reb forces wasn't enough. He started raidin' farms that he felt had been aidin' the Rebs. Some of the boys had a problem with burnin' out farmers, but Monroe had hung the last man to cross him, so everyone was afraid to say anything."

J.T. paused for a minute. Drew saw him look up and stare off into space. When he resumed his story, he did so in such a way that Drew felt as if he was watching the real events, not just listening to J.T. telling a story from years before. Drew closed his own eyes and could almost see the story unfold.

Monroe was riding lead with seven of the apostles following in a line. As usual, two men were hanging back making sure that they were not being followed and the two Vincent brothers from Pikeville were scouting ahead. No one said a word, and even the horses seemed to be moving through the woods without making a sound.

As the group topped the next hill, Joe Vincent was waiting for them. "Next two miles are clear, sir," the younger Vincent reported. "Nothing up ahead but a farm about a mile and half East of here."

Monroe thought for a minute. "That would be Butch Miller's place. His son, Keith, joined the Confederate Army last June. Corporal Vincent, ride back and find your brother, then circle around and approach the farm from the West."

Monroe then motioned for his men to move out. J.T. kicked his horse into a faster gate and rode up beside Monroe. "Colonel, We don't need supplies. Why are we goin' to the Miller place?"

Monroe never took his gaze off of the trail, "Sergeant, the book says, 'No man can serve two masters.' Mr. Miller's day of judgment has arrived."

J.T. knew that there was no arguing with Monroe once he had made a decision, so he fell back into line and waited to see how bad the situation would get. He prayed that no one would be there when they arrived.

As the group approached the farm it looked as if it was deserted, and J.T. thought that his prayer had been answered. He took one man and moved out to the left flank while two others rode to cover the right. J.T. noticed some movement between him and Monroe. "Fred, you stay here on the flank. I think there's somebody in that cornfield."

J.T. rode through the tall green stalks and found a young boy, no more than twelve, hiding in the field. He reached down and pulled the boy up onto his saddle. He did not think that Monroe would harm a boy, so he took him over to the Colonel.

J.T. let the kid down between his horse and Monroe's. "All we've found is this kid. Haven't seen hide or hair of anybody else."

Monroe gave the kid a cold stare and said, "Where is your father young man?"

When the boy did not respond Monroe reached down and slapped him hard across the face. "I asked you a question, boy. Are you going to answer me or should I give you a lesson on respecting your elders?"

The boy fought hard to keep a straight face and not to let the tears that had welled up in his eyes flow down his checks. "He's gone to town. Won't be back until tomorrow."

Monroe looked pleased. "Good. See that was not hard at all. Now, why did he go into town?"

When the boy did not answer right away Monroe lifted his hand as if to strike another blow. The boy flinched and then answered quickly, "He's gone to sell some beans and corn."

Monroe lowered his hand. "You mean he has gone to supply provisions to the Confederate Army."

"No, sir," the boy said, "we just had some left over after we put what we needed in the cellar. We need the money."

Monroe ignored the boy's response. "Mathews, bring the boy with us to the house. Sergeant Winters, inform the men to burn the field to deprive the enemy of any further provisions."

Mathews looked over at J.T. with a questioning look on his face. "Why are you looking to Sergeant Winters for clarification?" Monroe asked. "You have your orders."

Mathews knew not to press the point. He grabbed the boy by his collar and pulled him up onto his saddle.

J.T. watched as Monroe and Mathews rode toward the house with the boy. He had a feeling that something bad was going to come of the situation, but he also knew better than to question Monroe. Deep down some part of him knew what was about to happen. Furthermore, another part of him had already made the decision to stop it, even though he did not know how.

When J.T. saw Monroe throw a rope over one of the lower branches of the large oak tree in front of the house, he kicked his horse and rode toward Monroe at a full gallop. He almost knocked Mathews over with his horse before he pulled back on the reigns and swung down out of the saddle. He grabbed the boy's arm and pulled him from Monroe's grip. "What the hell are you doin'? He's just a boy; he ain't got nothin' to do with the war."

Monroe's eyes looked as if they had been replaced with the blackest of coal. "You forget yourself, Sergeant. Release the boy and carry out your orders."

"I won't let you do it. This time you've gone too far," J.T. said as he stood his ground.

"The Miller's have made their choice!" Monroe shouted. "Now let go of the boy and burn those fields."

J.T. drew his pistol and leveled it on Monroe's chest. "You're no officer, you're not even a preacher anymore, and, if you do this, you won't even be able to consider yourself a human being."

J.T. was so focused on Monroe and trying to stop him that he had forgotten about Mathews. When he heard the pistol cock behind him, J.T. made a fast half turn to his left and found himself face to face with Mathews, each man's gun was trained on the other. "Put it down. My fights not with you. You know this is wrong. Don't help him kill a boy." J.T. hoped that Mathews would come to his senses and help him stop Monroe from hanging a child for no reason.

J.T. did not see Monroe draw his sword, but he felt the blade slice deep into his right check. The blow caught him so much by surprise that he dropped his own weapon and grabbed his face. The cut ran from just under his eye to back toward his ear in a half circle and stopped just below his jaw. The flesh hung off his face exposing almost all of his check bone.

Monroe swung down out of his saddle saying, "You have betrayed me, Judas. I can not believe that you, my most trusted, would be the one to turn on me!"

J.T. tried to speak, but the words did not come. Everything was happening so fast. He looked down at himself and saw that his shirt was dripping with blood. It took him a second to real-ize that it was his own.

Monroe had moved around behind him. J.T. forced himself to clear his head. The Colonel was still talking. J.T. knew that he had to think of something fast.

"... I will say depart from me, yea never knew me." Then, J.T. felt the rope go around his neck. He reached to pull it away, but Monroe and Mathews had already begun to lift him from the ground. J.T. tried to turn toward them just as his feet were lifted into the air. Monroe was tying the rope off to one of the posts that supported the large porch that wrapped around three sides of the house. J.T.'s lungs felt as if they were going to explode. He watched as Monroe and Mathews mounted their horses and rode away. J.T. saw Monroe look back one final time just before the blackness moved in front of his eyes and the world drifted away into nothingness.

***

Drew realized that he had been so wrapped up in J.T.'s story that he was holding his breath and forced himself to take in a big gulp of air. J.T. looked up as if he was coming out of a trance. He shook his head, physically trying to clear his mind. "I guess in all the commotion the boy got away. Once Monroe and the rest of the men were gone, he came out of hiding and cut me down. I don't know why I lived, but I did."

"So what happened then?" Drew asked.

J.T. looked him in the eye for the first time since begin-ning his story and said, "I figured it would be best to skin-out. I headed west. I didn't really know how to do anything but kill, so I started makin' a living with my gun. I met up with a fella named Ringo, Johnny Ringo, and we started workin' for whoev-er was payin' the most for men who had a fast gun hand. There was good money to be made for gunslingers during the range wars down in Texas. Once things got to be a little more civilized down there, I worked cattle drives and sold my gun to whoever was buyin'. That was until I met my wife. Once I met her I put away my guns and left all the killin' behind me. Least, I thought I'd put it all behind me."

Drew shook his head and said, "I just don't get it. How come Monroe's still after you? That was all years ago."

J.T. laughed and said, "You don't know Monroe. In his way of thinking, I should be dead for crossin' him. As long as I'm breathin', I'm just a job he didn't finish. That's why he still travels with only eleven. The disciples didn't replace Judas as soon as he betrayed Jesus. They replaced him after he was dead. In Monroe's eyes, his Judas is still alive."

"So what is our next move?" Drew asked.

"I'm goin' to Hayes' ranch and kill that little son-of-a-bitch that murdered my family," J.T. responded.

Drew shook his head, "He ain't there. He let out after the John brought his Pa's body back to the ranch."

"Then I'm goin' after him and you're goin' back to help you're boss' son try and to keep Coven from runnin' him out," J.T. said. He thought that their next move was obvious.

Drew shook his head again, "That dog won't hunt. I'm goin' to kill Monroe. If you are too scared to face him, then I'll do it alone."

J.T. shot him a cold stare. "I like you, but if you ever call me yeller again I'll kill you for it."

Drew cleared his throat. "All I'm sayin' is that man has been huntin' you down for years. Why not end it while you have the chance."

Drew had a point. J.T. had been running from Monroe and his past for far too long. He had always hoped that sooner or later he would give up, but deep down he knew that Monroe would never stop until he saw J.T. dead. As much as he hated the idea of facing Monroe, he knew that the time had come to end it. He realized that if he was to ever have a future he would have to bury his past once and for all.

J.T. looked over at Drew and said, "Fine, but if we do this we do it my way. You do just what I tell you to and don't ask any questions. Is that clear?"

Drew nodded. "You got it. You're the boss."

J.T. stood up and said, "Clean and load your guns. Now this is how it's going to go down."

CHAPTER 6

Olenger rode up to the Hayes ranch. To his surprise, no one tried to stop him. John Hayes stood waiting for him on the front porch of the main house with a rifle cradled across his chest. Olenger realized that he must have been seen, but was not stopped because he was alone.

John spoke first, "You can take your threats right back to your boss. Tell him that even though my father is dead, that does not mean that I'm going to roll over to his demands."

"I'm not here to cause more trouble. Coven said to tell you things have gotten out of hand. He's runnin' off them killers he hired. He wants you to come to our ranch to sit down and hammer things out. He said that you could bring whoever you wanted. You have my word this ain't no trap. I'll take my oath on it."

John wanted to believe him, but something in the back of his mind kept telling him that this *was* some kind of trick. However, this just might be his chance to end the range war once and for all. He wished that his father was here now to help him decide what to do. The old man had always been hard on him. John had hated him for it most of his life, but now he realized how much he had loved and respected his father. He wished that he could have told the old man how he felt. He wanted to tell him that he understood why he had been so hard, but now he would never have the chance. The only thing that he could do for Al Hayes now was to keep the ranch going. John knew that the best way to do that was to end the war with Coven.

"O.K.," John finally responded, "but, I'm bringing some of my men with me and they will be armed."

Olenger smiled and said, "I don't care how you come, just as long as you come."

John told the man standing closest to him to inform the rest of the ranch hands what was happening and then motioned for the remainder of the men who had gathered to saddle their horses and follow him. If this was a trick and he was going to die, he knew that at least Becky would be close by. John thought that he could face anything as long as he knew that she was there with him.

***

Monroe entered Coven's study rather annoyed at having been summoned while he was going over his plans to finally kill J.T. Winters. He saw Coven sitting behind his desk obviously trying to look as stern as possible. Monroe wondered how long the pompous fool had taken to gather enough courage to speak to him. Regardless of Coven's attempt to not look afraid, his fear was manifest in the fact that Bell was standing in the corner of the room to Monroe's left and rear. At least Coven was not a total fool.

"Mr. Monroe," Coven began, "your services will no longer be needed. My initial goals have been accomplished. Your money is there on the serving bar. I expect you and your men to be off my property within the hour."

Monroe looked over at the bar to his right. Coven had planned this through in detail. The money was not on his desk, which would have put them close enough to each other for Monroe to kill him before Bell could react.

"We will remain on your property until we have completed our mission. I have unfinished business to see to." Monroe watched Coven for his reaction. Coven's expression did not change; apparently he had already planned for Monroe's refusal to leave.

"Very well, I only ask that you leave as soon as possible. You and your men are no longer welcome here," Coven said.

Monroe turned and exited the room without saying another word, and without picking up the money. Coven and Bell waited to hear the front door close.

"I guess that settles it," Bell said.

Coven lowered his head. "It certainly does. Are the men ready?"

"The lookouts are in place watchin' their bunkhouse," Bell answered "The rest are waitin' for the word from you to move into position."

Coven looked up and said, "Put two of the men with my wife and daughter in the cellar. Inform them to remain there until it is done. Then meet me in the barn."

Bell nodded in response and exited the house. Coven retrieved his Springfield from the gun case and a box of shells from his desk. There was little time to waste. Coven knew that he must finish cleaning up this mess before Olenger returned with John Hayes.

Coven entered the barn and faced his men. "Is everyone clear on what they are expected to do. I know that these men are professionals, but we have superior numbers and we will prevail."

Bell entered the barn and leaned in close to Coven's ear so as not to be heard by the other men. "The women folk are in the cellar with two men watching the door."

"Then it is time," Coven announced. "Everyone move into position."

Coven and Bell moved out with the rest of the men and

took their positions behind a buckboard roughly thirty-feet from the front of the bunkhouse. Coven waited for everyone to signal that they were ready before he began to speak.

"Mr. Monroe," Coven yelled at the bunkhouse. "My men have you surrounded. Please evacuate my property immediately, or we will have no other option but to force you to leave."

Coven waited for a response, but no one answered.

Coven tried again, "I will not ask again. Please come out and leave my land now."

Bell could not believe that Coven had the nerve to be so polite even when threatening to kill someone. He knew that Monroe would see Coven's politeness as a sign of weakness. Bell also knew that the only way to deal with a situation like this one was to be forceful and to not hesitate. If Monroe was going to leave of his own free will he would have done so when Coven had asked him to in the house.

The men inside of the bunkhouse had extinguished almost all of the lanterns when Coven first announced their presence. The best Bell could tell there was only one lantern still burning. Once the men inside had moved into their defensive positions, that one would be put out also. Bell saw a silhouette move in front of one of the windows and saw it as his best opportunity. He fired a single shot at the figure and saw the outline of the man fall to the floor. Within seconds, everyone had opened fire.

Coven turned to Bell. "I did not give the order to fire!"

Bell ignored him and continued to send lead hurdling toward the structure. Coven just watched as the small bunkhouse was riddled with bullets. All of the windows were shattered and the front door was almost completely blown off its hinges. The men inside did not have time to extinguish the last of the lanterns. It continued to burn until one of the hundreds of bullets being sent into the building struck the lantern causing the bunkhouse to burst into flames.

Bell was impressed with how hard the men inside of the bunkhouse fought back and with the accuracy of their fire. He watched as several of the cowhands fell to the ground. Most had never been in a gunfight and were not properly taking advantage of their cover. As the fire continued to burn, the amount of shots being fired from inside began to subside. Bell also realized that Coven had not fired a single round. As usual, he was leaving the dirty work to someone else. Bell scanned the area and saw that all of the men within sight of his position had been killed or had their complete attention focused on their wounds.

Bell turned to Coven and said, "I always wanted to tell you, no one likes a smart ass know-it-all." He then fired a single shot at point-blank range. The round exited the back of Coven's skull, taking most of the contents of his head with it. Bell grinned, rather pleased with how the events had come to pass. With Coven, Hayes, and Monroe all dead, Bell was looking forward to a large reward and two ranches; he would never have to lift another finger as long as he lived.

Only a few sporadic shots were now being fired at the bunkhouse, and no rounds were being returned from inside of the burning structure. The entire battle had lasted only a few minutes, although, it had seemed like much longer. Bell waited a few moments longer to see if the fire would force out anyone who might still be alive inside. When he was satisfied that Monroe and his men were dead, we walked from behind the buckboard and stood facing what was left of the front door.

The surviving ranch hands soon joined him. Bell counted only eleven others who had come through the fight without serious wounds. His first order of business as ranch owner would be to take care of Coven's wife and daughter so they would not claim the ranch for themselves. Bell knew that if he did not kill them, Becky would believe that she could run the ranch herself.

But once she was out of the picture, he would have to hire some more help. There was no way he could run two ranches with only eleven hands. He did not even have enough men left to run John Hayes off his father's place. However, there would be time to worry about the small details later.

Bell turned to the two men to his right and said, "You two check the bunkhouse. Make sure that they're all dead."

"Where's Coven?" the man closest to him asked.

"Dead," Bell responded. "Now do what I told you to do and quit stallin'."

The two men carefully approached the building. One man kicked down what remained of the door while the other covered him. After a few moments, they returned with their report. "I see five bodies, but the whole back half of the bunkhouse is in flames," the man who kicked the door in reported. "The rest may be back there."

The man giving the report grabbed his chest and fell to the ground before Bell realized that he had heard the shot. One more man fell dead before the group could turn around to return fire. Monroe had somehow managed to escape out the back of the Bunkhouse with six of his men. They had circled around behind Bells group of survivors and had now opened fire on them from behind.

Ten against seven would have been good odds in a gunfight, if the seven had not been professionals. After a few seconds of exchanging shots, Bell's advantage was gone. He was now facing Monroe and four of his Disciples, while Bell had only himself and three ranch hands. Bell threw his gun to the ground and raised his hands, his men quickly followed suit.

"Don't shoot!" Bell exclaimed. "We was only doin' what Coven told us to. We didn't want to fight to begin with. We had nothin' to do with this."

Monroe and his men advanced on the survivors, and surrounded them.

***

J.T. and Drew had dismounted their horses and were approaching the Coven ranch on foot when they heard another bust of gunfire. The light from the burning bunkhouse illuminated the area quite well. J.T. could see bodies strewn around the burning building. He breathed a sigh of relief when he only counted four men with Monroe; maybe he and Drew actually stood a chance at pulling this off.

J.T. whispered to Drew, "Change of plans. You stay here with the rifle and cover me. They'll expect me to be alone. No matter what, you stay here. If things go bad, cut out for Hayes' place."

Drew nodded his understanding and got down into a prone position to best steady his shot. J.T. moved in closer and could now hear part of what was being said.

Monroe was the one speaking, "Drop to your knees and prepare for an eternity of Hell-fire and damnation."

One man was doing all the talking for the surrounded men. J.T. could not hear what he was saying, but apparently he was crying like an infant and begging for his life. Monroe and his remaining Disciples then raised their weapons and executed the four men.

Monroe turned to his four remaining men, "Finish off the wounded, and then search the house for Coven's wife and daughter. Use caution, Coven was careful enough to have left them under the protection of armed guards."

J.T. stepped from the darkness and into the light of the burning bunkhouse. "I can't let you hurt the women folks. They had nothin' to do with this."

67

Monroe's men immediately stepped between their leader and J.T.

"Mathews, you and rest of ya'll are free to go. This is between me and the Colonel," J.T. said.

Drew could not hear what was being said, but he could see that J.T. was now faced off with four men. Drew took careful aim at the man closest to him and prepared to fire. Seconds later, he saw everyone reach for their guns and he squeezed the trigger dropping the man in his sites. He then jumped to his feet and advanced on the group as quickly as he could while he chambered another round into the rifle. The man next to the one he had just shot instinctively turned to face the direction from which the shot had come. Drew leveled his sites on the man now facing him and pulled the trigger. The man fell to his knees and then toppled face first to the ground, but not before he got off a shot of his own. Drew felt the bullet rip through his left thigh and he fell hard face first into the ground knocking him unconscious.

***

J.T. knew that Drew would fire at the man to his far left first being that he was closest to Drew's position. J.T. then focused on the two men to his right. When he saw the men reach for their weapons, J.T. drew both of his guns and fired them simultaneously. The man to his far left fell from Drew's shot just a split second before the two men in his sights fell backwards to the ground. However, Mathews was able to get off a round just as he was hit that struck J.T. in the upper left arm causing him to drop the Navy Colt that he was training onto the remaining man in the line. Luckily, that man had turned to face Drew instead of J.T. The man fell to his knees just after firing a shot in Drew's direction. J.T. heard a scream form just beyond the light of the fire, and did not hear any more movement from Drew's direction. He would have to finish this by himself.

Now, for the first time in years, J.T. found himself standing face to face with Monroe. The light from the fire behind Monroe cast shadows on his face that made him look almost demonic. J.T. tried hard to focus on Monroe and block out the shearing pain in his left arm.

Monroe was the first to speak, "So the wages of your sin was the death of all of my men."

"I'm not the sinner here," J.T. said. "You're the one who kills women and children."

"I merely judge the wicked," Monroe responded.

J.T. sighed and said, "It's not your job to judge the wicked. That job is God's and his alone. You used to understand that."

"God sent me on this mission to purge the world of evil. Who am I to question the will of God?" Monroe asked.

"'God didn't send you on any mission!" J.T. exclaimed. "I was the one who asked you to fight back, remember? I thought men would follow you because you were a leader in the community. The whole idea about how many men to use and how to fight back was mine. I was the one who created the monster that you've become."

Monroe smiled and said, "Then how can you judge me when from the beginning all you cared about was revenge for your brother's death?"

"Jimmy was your brother too. If I had known then that by askin' you to lead us that I would wind up losin' you too, I would never have asked. Now I have one brother whose dead and another that might as well be." J.T. waited for Monroe to draw his pistol. During the war, if anyone mentioned that J.T. and Monroe were brothers, Monroe would go into a rage. He did not want anyone to believe that J.T. received any kind of special

treatment. That is why he always sent J.T. on the most dangerous missions.

However, Monroe did not go for his gun, instead he lowered his head. "I know. I wanted revenge as much as you did,
but killing the ones who killed Jimmy was not enough. I wanted
more. Then you had the courage to try and stop the cycle of
death that we had created. I hated you for that. That day showed
me that I was beyond salvation. I knew that I would never be
able to..."

"It's not too late," J.T. said as he holstered the gun he still
held in his right hand. "You can start over. I did. I found a wife
and settled down. You can start a new life. You can finally stop
fightin'. The war is over."

Monroe quickly drew his pistol and aimed it at J.T.'s chest.
"No! I have to finish what I have started. I have chosen my path;
there is no forgiveness for what I have done."

"You'll have to kill me then," J.T. responded as he lifted his
hands. "I won't fight you."

J.T. could see the mussel of Monroe's gun shacking. He
obviously was having second thoughts about gunning down his
own brother in cold blood. J.T. started to speak, but could not
find the words. If Monroe killed him, at least he would be with
Kaye and Mark again. He closed his eyes and he could almost
picture them standing in a field of wildflowers waiting for him.
Then, J.T. heard the sound of the gun firing.

It took him a second to gather himself enough to notice
that he was still standing. He opened his eyes and saw Monroe
lying on the ground in front of him. That was when J.T. realized
that the sound of the shot had come from his left. Drew came
limping up from out of the darkness using his rifle as a crutch.

J.T. fell to his knees and cradled Monroe's head in his

hands. He wiped the blood from his brother's mouth as Monroe looked up at him. "I'm…I'm…"

"Don't try to talk. Hold on and I'll get you some help," J.T. said.

"No," Monroe said in a low raspy voice that came out as little more than a whisper. "It is my appointed time."

J.T. shook his head and said, "No, you hang on. You can make it through this, and we can start all over where nobody knows who we are or what we've done."

Monroe struggled to breath. "Jeremiah, forgive me. I'm sorry." Then he took one last breath and was gone.

J.T. was surprised that he felt relieved. Not that Monroe was dead, but that he had finally seen his brother, the brother that he remembered from before the war. J.T. had seen the man that he had once loved in Monroe's eyes just before he died. Somehow, he knew that when Monroe had asked for forgiveness, J.T. had not been the only one that he was asking to forgive him. Monroe Winters was in a better place.

"I'm sorry," Drew said. "I had no idea."

J.T. closed his brother's eyes and gently placed his head on the ground, "It's O.K. You finally released him. Maybe he can find the peace in death that he could never find in life." J.T. fought hard to hold back the flood of emotions. Not only for Monroe, but also for Jimmy, Kaye, Mark, and the sea of faces that J.T. saw in his dreams. Faces of men he had sent to early graves. How many of them had had wives, children, and brothers?

J.T. and Drew both turned at the sound of the approaching horses. They saw Onlenger and John Hayes surveying the carnage. J.T. stood and picked up his Colt that was still lying on the ground and holstered it.

Olenger looked down at J.T. and asked, "What the hell happened?"

"Best I can tell, Coven tried to force Monroe and his men to leave. We didn't get here till it was nearly over," J.T. answered.

John swung down out of his saddle and ran for the main house screaming, "Becky! Becky!"

Becky burst from the cellar door pulling herself free from one of Coven's men who had her by the arm. "I'm here! John, over here!" The two young lovers ran into each other's arms.

Olivia Coven came out of the cellar calling for her husband. When he did not respond, she walked toward the burning embers that were once a bunkhouse until she found his body. She sat down beside his remains and began to cry. Becky and John walked over to comfort the grieving widow.

"So if it is over, who won?" Olenger asked.

"No one," J.T. said. "No one ever wins."

CHAPTER 7

Missouri Jake had only been in Denver for two days, but he had already found a job. He had been hired to kill a gambler named Ben Madison. He figured the best place to look for a gambler was in a saloon, so he strolled into the biggest one on Main Street. He walked around the smoke filled room cluttered with drunks, gamblers, and whores.

Not seeing anyone who fit the description of Madison, he decided to sit down at a poker table and ask a few questions. He waited until the players were done with their present hand, and then asked if he could join them. When they agreed, he took a seat and laid his money on the table. The dealer coughed violently into a handkerchief then looked up at Jake and asked, "So, who do I have the pleasure of depriving of their hard earned money this evening?"

The dealer's thick southern accent was stronger than any that Jake had ever heard. "Names Jake."

"It's a pleasure young Jake," he said tipping his hat. He then placed his five dollars into the center of the table and dealt the cards.

Jake looked at his hand. "So do any of you know a fella named Ben Madison?"

The man to his right asked for three cards, then answered, "Yea. He's upstairs with one of the girls. I guess he couldn't wait to spend some of his winnins."

Jake was so happy that Madison was in the saloon that he almost folded his hand before he realized he was holding four queens with a king kicker. He pushed all of his money into the pot and said, "You boys will have to pay to see this hand."

The dealer smiled and said, "Must be a peach of a hand." He then took a drink and looked deep into Jake's eyes. "I just can't help myself; I have to call." He then pushed his own money to the center of the table.

Jake laughed out loud. "Sorry mister, looks like I'm the one taken your hard earned money this evening." He slowly laid his cards out one at a time, then reached for the pot.

"Not so fast," the dealer said. "That is a peach of a hand, but I do believe that this one is better." He then laid down his own cards revealing a Jack high straight flush."

Jake shot up out of his chair, but before he could reach for his gun, the dealer had already drawn his own. Jake was amazed at the speed of the skinny pale looking man.

The man to his right tried to diffuse the situation. "There's nothin' to be mad about son. You ain't the first man to lose a hand or to be outdrawn by Doc Holliday."

"Doc Holliday?" Jake was stunned. He began walking backwards slowly. "I didn't come here to play cards anyhow. You said Madison was upstairs right. I better go on and find him."

Holliday holstered his gun as Jake turned and walked upstairs. A few moments later, he heard a gunshot over the sound of the piano. He later learned that the kid had shot Mr. Madison in the back of the head and then escaped though an upstairs window.

***

Dr. White paced back and forth in front of the door trying one last time to make Mossman change his mind. "We need you here. We have to have a Sheriff. What will the town do while you are gone?"

Mossman continued to get dressed. "Tony Keys will be acting Sheriff while I'm gone. I have to bring that man in."

Dr. White stopped pacing and said, "That man is a hired killer. You're good Steve, but he's better. And, you only have one arm now. How are you going to bring him in?"

"I don't know," the Sheriff answered. "But I can't let that man walk into town, kill my brother, shoot me, and then just let him go like nothing ever happened. If I did I could never look anyone in the face again. Hell, I wouldn't even be able to look at myself in mirror."

Dr. White sat down on the corner of the bed and said, "If you go after him, he'll kill you. You can't beat him."

Mossman looked over at his friend, "There are certain things that a man has to do or he can't call himself a man. I'm going to find J.T. Winters. And when I do, I'm going to bring him back. Dead or Alive, I don't care which."

***

Drew helped J.T. saddle his horse. J.T. did not like having another man help him with his horse, but with his left arm in a sling he did not have much of a choice. He had been lucky, the bullet passed through his bicep without touching the bone. Within no time it would be just another scar.

"You know that you could stay here with us if you wanted," Becky said as she handed him some food for his journey.

"Thank you," J.T. said as he placed the food into his saddlebag, "but I have to be goin'"

John Hayes reached for J.T.'s hand. "If you ever need anything, you know where we are."

J.T. shook the young man's hand. "Much obliged. You just take care of that girl and her Ma." John nodded in response and then walked back to the house hand in hand with Becky.

Drew finished tightening the girth strap on J.T.'s saddle. "You know she's right. You don't have to go after the kid."

"I reckon I do," J.T. responded. "I can't just let it go like nothin' happened."

"In that case, like John said, if you ever need anything at all you know where you can find me," Drew said.

J.T. shook his friend's hand, then saddled his horse and rode west. The sun was setting and he could not remember the last time that he had been alone out on the plains. He had always loved the peace and quiet of the open range. J.T. thought about Kaye and Mark. He hoped that they were not lonely without him. He wished that he could hold them one more time. He wanted to kiss his wife, play with his son, and tell them that he was sorry that they had paid for what he had done before they had ever met. He also thought about his brothers. He knew that they would look after his family until he could join them.

Then, he suddenly wondered if he would ever see them again. If he continued after Missouri Jake, if he continued to kill, to decide who was worthy to live and who was not, was he any better than the monster that Monroe had become? His brother had been given the chance to find redemption. What if the bullet that was meant to end J.T.'s life did not give him the opportunity to ask for forgiveness?

Was it too late? Was he now more monster than man? J.T. Winters did not know if he would find forgiveness for his sins. He did not even know what he would do if he ever caught the boy who had killed his family. All he knew to do was to continue the search. He only hoped that he could live with the answers, if he ever found them.